619   30p

POCKET · PUFFINS

D1136308

To the Ashes

Puffin Books, Penguin Books Ltd, Harmondsworth, Middlesex, England
Viking Penguin Inc., 40 West 23rd Street, New York, New York 10010, U.S.A.
Penguin Books Australia Ltd, Ringwood, Victoria, Australia
Penguin Books Canada Limited, 2801 John Street, Markham, Ontario, Canada L3R 1B4
Penguin Books (N.Z.) Ltd, 182-190 Wairau Road, Auckland 10, New Zealand

Puffin/Moonlight
First published by Jonathan Cape Ltd 1980
Text copyright © Russell Hoban, 1978
Illustrations copyright © Quentin Blake, 1980
Published in Pocket Puffins 1987 in association with Moonlight Publishing Ltd,
131 Kensington Church Street, London W8

Printed in Italy by La Editoriale Libraria

The Twenty-Elephant Restaurant

Text by Russell Hoban
Pictures by Quentin Blake

POCKET PUFFINS

A man and a woman lived in a little house. They had a bed and a table and two chairs. The bed was good and the chairs were good but the table wobbled. The man always had to put a book of matches under one leg, sometimes under two. After a while the matchbooks would disappear and he would have to get new ones.

7

When Christmas came, the man gave the woman a handkerchief and she gave him a tie. They sat down at the table and said, "Merry Christmas."

"It doesn't feel like Christmas," said the woman.

"No wonder," said the man.

"What do you mean?" said the woman.

"This table," said the man.

"What about the table?" said the woman.

"It's wearing me out," said the man.

8

The woman shook her head. All day she walked around shaking her head.

That evening at supper the man said to her, "Why are you shaking your head?"

"It isn't right," she said. "It's wrong."

"What's wrong?" he said.

"The way things are with you and that table," said the woman. "It's all right for a man to wear out a table, but a table shouldn't wear out a man."

"It was just a manner of speaking," said the man. "I didn't really mean that the table is wearing me out."

"I've been thinking about it all day," said the woman. "Before we got that table you were young and handsome. Now you're old and ugly. What you said was true. That table is wearing you out."

"But we've had the table for fifty years," said the man. "It stands to reason I'm not as young and handsome as I was fifty years ago."

"Whether it stands to reason we don't know," said the woman. "All we know is how it was before the table and how it is now."

"What do you think I should do?" said the man.

"It isn't for me to say," said the woman.

"Say it anyhow," said the man.

"I think you should make a new table," said the woman.

"*Make* one?" said the man. "I've never *made* a table. We bought the old one."

"Look at the wrapped bread they sell nowadays," said the woman. "Look at the chemicals they put in chickens. Look at pollution. How can you expect to buy a good table?"

"You're right," said the man. "I'll find a tablewood tree and I'll cut it down and saw it up and I'll make a new table."

"I'm glad you've decided to do that," said the woman. "I think that's a wise decision."

The man went into the woods and found a good straight-grained tablewood tree. He cut it down and sawed it up. He stacked the wood and left it to season for a couple of years.

Every so often he turned it over so that it would not warp. He could hardly wait to make the table, and when the wood was well seasoned he measured it off and sawed it to size. He drilled holes and pegged it together and made the table. He planed it smooth and he sanded it down and there it was, a new table.

"That really is a young, handsome, strong new table," said the man. "The old table was wearing me out, but this

12

one is building me up."

"You look much better," said the woman. "You look fifty years younger already. There's nothing like a new table."

"You're absolutely right," said the man. "And that table is really strong. It's steady as a rock. No matchbooks under that table. Elephants could dance on that table."

"How many?" said the woman.

"Only one really," said the man. "I don't think there's room for two."

"Oh," said the woman. "When you said elephants, I thought you meant more than one."

"One to a table, I'd say," said the man. "I could make more tables for that matter. There's lots of wood left from the tree I cut down."

"Where would we get the elephants?" said the woman.

"Advertise in the Classified Section," said the man. "Elephants wanted for table work. Must be agile."

"Then we'd have to pay them," said the woman.

"If people paid to see them dance, then we could pay the elephants," said the man.

"How do you know they'll be worth paying to see?" said the woman. "Maybe they won't be good enough dancers."

"We could open a restaurant," said the man. "The elephants could wait on the tables, and in their spare time they could practise dancing until they're good enough so people will pay to see them."

"They'll need a dancing instructor," said the woman.

"We can work it out as we go along," said the man. "The first thing is more tables." He measured and sawed and drilled and pegged and planed and sanded night and day, and he made seventeen more tables, all of them as strong and steady as the first one and none of them needing matchbooks under the legs.

When he'd made the tables, he couldn't
get them all inside the little house.
Even with tables standing on top of
tables, seven of them had to wait outside.

"A tent?" said the woman.

"Elephants and a tent make a
circus," said the man. "And I'm not
having a circus. I just want a straight
restaurant with dancing elephants."

"Chairs," said the woman.

"Right," said the man. "We've got
eighteen tables now, and four chairs
to a table makes seventy-two chairs.

We already have two chairs so I just
have to make seventy more. I can't
wait to see the whole thing put
together. The eighteen tables and the
eighteen elephants waiting on them
and dancing and the seventy-two
people sitting on the chairs in the
restaurant."

"And a chef," said the woman.
"I can cook for two people but not
for seventy-two."

"Right," said the man. "When I advertise for the elephants, I'll put in the ad: Dancing and cooking experience helpful."

"Bookkeeping," said the woman. "After all, it's a business."

"Dancing, cooking and book-keeping experience," said the man. He put the advertisement in the local newspaper:

Elephants wanted for table work. Must be agile. Dancing, cooking and bookkeeping experience helpful.

Then he went into the woods and cut down four restaurantwood trees and two chairwood trees. He sawed up the wood and he stacked it and he left it to season for a couple of years.

Meanwhile they began to get telephone calls from elephants. The first elephant who called was not agile and he could not dance, cook or keep books. But he was an experienced truck driver.

"I'll hire him," said the man. "If things get slow, we can fill in with long-distance trucking."

"And truck drivers always like a good place to eat, and they tell their friends," said the woman. "So that'll bring in new customers."

The man hired the elephant and went into the woods and cut down a truckwood tree. He sawed it up and left the wood to season.

The next elephant who rang them up was a dancing instructor. The one after that was a cook. The one after that was a bookkeeper. All of them were agile.

"That's four," said the man. "Now we only need fourteen more elephants."

"Fifteen," said the woman. "We need nineteen altogether. Eighteen for

the tables and one in the kitchen."

Fifteen more elephants rang up. All of them were agile and interested in table work.

"Now we're all set," said the man.

"While we're waiting for the wood to season the elephants can practise their dancing and we'll be in good shape when it's time to open the restaurant."

The telephone rang. It was another elephant.

"We've already got nineteen elephants," said the man. "We don't need any more."

"Nineteen is a funny number," said the elephant on the telephone. "With twenty you can call it 'The Twenty-Elephant Restaurant.'"

"Are you agile?" said the man.

"No," said the elephant. "But I'm reliable."

"All right," said the man. "You're hired."

The twentieth elephant made road signs for the restaurant. He went out and put up a sign every ten miles on all the roads for a hundred miles in all directions. Every sign told how far it was to: The Twenty-Elephant Restaurant.

The twentieth elephant was out putting up signs for two years while the other elephants practised dancing. When he got back, there was a line of cars and trucks ten miles long waiting for the restaurant to open.

By then the chairwood and the restaurantwood and the truckwood were well enough seasoned, so the man got to work. First he made the seventy chairs.

As soon as the chairs were finished everybody got out of the trucks and cars. Seventy-two of them pulled the chairs up to the tables and sat down. "Where's the restaurant?" they said.

"I'm building it now," said the man.

He started sawing and hammering
while everybody watched him. Those
who had chairs sat down and watched
and those who didn't have chairs
stood and watched.

"Don't watch me," said the man.
"Watch the elephants."

The eighteen elephant waiters all
got up on the tables and started to
dance.

"Down in front!" everybody said to the elephants. "Get off the tables, you're blocking our view."

"Don't you want to see us dance?" said the elephants. "We've been practising every day for two years."

"Get down!" everybody shouted. "We can't see what he's doing."

"Nothing goes right for me," said the man. "I start out to have a twenty-elephant restaurant and I wind up being a one-man circus."

"It's only temporary," said the woman. "Don't do any more until we collect admission money and sell some hot dogs."

The twentieth elephant quickly made a sign:

"You'd better make that 50p *daily* admission," said the man. "It's going to take me two weeks to build this restaurant."

So they changed the sign and they

collected 50p from everybody. Then
the elephant chef made hot dogs, and
the elephant waiters danced around
and sold them.

The man built the restaurant and
wired it and put in the plumbing and
installed the kitchen. He painted and
stained and varnished and he
screwed in the light bulbs and hooked
up the music. It took him two weeks
to finish the restaurant.

Everybody stayed to watch for the
whole two weeks, and they paid 50p
and ate hot dogs every day.

When the restaurant was finished,
he turned on the music and he turned
on the sign and it flashed on and off.

Everybody clapped and cheered, and
the man bowed. Then everybody went
into the restaurant and had a meal.

While they were eating, the man took the truckwood and he built an enormous truck.

"What's that for?" said the woman. "We don't need a truck now. The restaurant is a big success and we won't have to do any long-distance trucking."

"I don't take anything for granted any more," said the man.

There were long lines of cars and

trucks at the restaurant every day.
The elephant chef was cooking and the
elephant dancing instructor was
working up new routines, the elephant
waiters were dancing on the tables
before and after every meal and the
elephant bookkeeper was adding up
big profits. The dancing instructor
taught the twentieth elephant to
dance too, so everybody was busy all
the time.

One evening one of the customers said, "Why is my cream-of-chicken soup sliding back and forth in the bowl?"

The elephant waiter called the man over. The man looked at the table carefully and he checked every leg separately. The table was as steady as a rock. While he was checking the table a customer at another table said,

"Why is my jelly quivering like that?"

The man checked the other table. That one too was as steady as a rock. He went to a corner of the restaurant and shifted his weight from one foot to the other. Everything on all the tables wobbled.

"Matchbook?" said the woman.

"No," said the man. "I'm not having that."

He took the restaurant apart
and the elephants loaded it into the
truck. The man and the woman and all
the elephants got in, the truck driver
elephant started the truck and they
drove off.

"Where to?" said the truck driver
elephant.

"Somewhere flat," said the man.

When they found a flat place, the
twenty elephants went out and moved
all the road signs so they told how far
it was to the new location. Then they
put up the sign that said:

Mr BUILDO
The One-Man Circus!

See Mr Buildo
build a Restaurant
Single-handed!
Admission DAILY 50p

Enjoy a hot dog
cooked and served
by dancing
elephants

They collected admission money
and they sold hot dogs and the man
put the restaurant together again.
Business was good and they stayed
until the restaurant started to wobble.
Then they moved on.

"Maybe there aren't any places
that'll stay flat," said the woman.

"Maybe that's just how it is."

"I think maybe you're right," said the man. "Sometimes it's a one-man circus and sometimes it's a twenty-elephant restaurant. And that's life."

"Still," said the elephants, "it's not a bad life."

"No," said the man, "it isn't."

RUSSELL HOBAN, an American living in London, is one of the best-known and most popular authors of children's books writing today. He has published over thirty-five books for children, including the modern classic, *The Mouse and His Child*.

His long-standing collaboration with Quentin Blake dates back to *Captain Najork and His Hired Sportsmen*. It is a partnership of which Quentin Blake has spoken with enthusiasm: "I think Russell Hoban is one of the best writers for children, one with an intimate knowledge of the sound and shape of language."

QUENTIN BLAKE is an outstanding and prolific illustrator. He has illustrated well over a hundred books, including *Mouse Trouble*, *The Enormous Crocodile*, and *The BFG*, along with stories such as *The Dancing Frog* and *Mr Magnolia*, which he has written himself. As well as all this, he teaches in the Illustration Department at the Royal College of Art, encouraging young illustrators. He sees author, illustrator and reader as mutually stimulating one another, and loves the direct response he gets when he encounters groups of children in libraries, schools and bookshops.